BLOODMOON

A SHORT STORY PREQUEL TO
THE BANE OF YOTO

BLOODMOON

BIRTH OF THE BEAST

NEW YORK TIMES BESTSELLING AUTHOR

KEITH FERRELL

HEX PUBLISHERS

BLOODMOON: BIRTH OF THE BEAST

Written by Keith Ferrell
Copyedits by Bret Smith and Jeanni Smith
Cover illustrations by Damonza.com
Interior illustrations by Branden Bendert and Stephen B. Scott
Keith Ferrell portrait by Aaron Lovett
Typesets and formatting by Alec Ferrell

A Hex Publishers Book

Published & Distributed by Hex Publishers, LLC
PO BOX 298
Erie, CO 80516

www.HexPublishers.com

Joshua Viola, Publisher

Paperback ISBN: 979-8-9862194-6-2
e-Book ISBN: 979-8-9862194-7-9
December 2022

10 9 8 7 6 5 4 3 2 1

Printed in the U.S.A.

In loving memory of

Keith Ferrell
1953–2020

Good work. We miss you, Mon.

T HERE HAD BEEN THREE OTHERS with Vega in his mother's wombsac. Whether they were to be brothers or sisters he did not know, nor did he care. Male or female, they would be rivals and that, even before birth, he did care about. Deeply.

He devoured his siblings one by one, taking his time. There was no hurry—there was no place for the others to hide from his appetite.

When he was born, no hint of the others remained. Only Vega emerged.

Some of the attendants present said the newborn was the largest olokun infant they had ever seen; his birthclaws were the most fully formed of any olokun in history.

All swore the infant's eyes narrowed and sharpened when those surrounding the birthing spoke. Some claimed the eyes glowed slightly with a whiteness of light none had ever seen.

"Born to rule," they said.

When word of their comments reached Master Trusk, the closest thing to a unifier the various olokun tribes and clans possessed, it was said the old olokun chuckled, but his laughter was laced with fear.

The first time Vega tasted numah blood, the rich, dark liquid brought to him by an attendant not long after he was born, he lapped happily at the bowl until it was empty.

By the time Ajyin completed a full cycle around its star, Vega was speaking. With his first words, he demanded numah blood…a demand he repeated as frequently as Telya would permit him to have it.

Before Vega had seen Ajyin complete two cycles, he tasted the blood of a numah killed and shredded with his own claws. He discovered the flavor was richer, more complex, far more satisfying when the blood flowed fresh from wounds he created. It tasted…alive. Vega savored the taste and allowed its fullness to flow through him as he dreamed of future kills.

Still too young to know much, Vega already knew more than his age should have allowed, and far more than he allowed others to be aware of. Like his claws, Vega's instincts were fully formed before he emerged from his mother—and the most sharply refined of those instincts was wariness.

Belfang studied the numah village from the

crest of a hill. His finest, fiercest warriors were arrayed to both sides of his observation point, with reserves clustered in the valley behind them. Belfang never had need to call upon reserve troops, nor did he expect to summon them to battle now, despite the size of the village. This was close to being the largest he ever assaulted, perhaps twenty separate structures.

Yet Belfang felt no more apprehension than he had when descending upon clusters of two or three numah huts that were the typical intrusion of their species upon his. The difference to Belfang was one only of degree, not danger—dozens of numah posed no more challenge to him than did a scant handful of the furred creatures.

He thought, in fact, he could deal with the entire population of this village himself, with only the force of his two claws. For a moment, he thought he would do so, and nearly rose from his vantage point to launch himself upon them.

But if there are privileges that come with leadership, there are also self-denials. Belfang knew the troops accompanying him were eager to prove themselves. A true leader would deny himself before denying his warriors, and Belfang was determined to be known as a true leader. More than that—he wished to be respected and revered. That wish, and the ambition that underlay it, guided many of his actions.

Belfang signaled for his soldiers to make their weapons ready, but to hold themselves in position until the moment was right. He sharpened his gaze upon the numah settlement, and as he did so, he thought of his child.

Before many more cycles passed, Vega would be old enough to accompany Belfang on hunting trips and, not long after that, on the occasional punitive expeditions against the numah. Such missions were actually quite rare—one every cycle or two. The numah kept mostly to themselves and their own lands. An uneasy, wary distance usually separated the two species, punctuated by occasional confrontations, but also by small economic exchanges.

The attack Belfang was now preparing to launch was unusual, as was the size of the numah community below him. The problem was that the creatures bred so rapidly. Their numbers seemed to double every cycle. Or even more frequently than that, Belfang reflected as he saw yet another cluster of numah younglings emerge from one of the huts they called homes. He supposed it was appropriate that beings capable of living in such structures be equally repellant in how quickly their population grew. It took many numah to fashion structures that were built, not grown; that were assembled from wood and stone and mud rather than created of living tissue. Every aspect of the numah violated the natural and correct order of things, Belfang thought.

And still he did not move against them unless they transgressed against olokun property and olokun rights—otherwise their relationship to the natural order of things was their business, as Belfang saw it. Like Master Trusk—like many olokun—Belfang felt the numah had a purpose and did not discourage minor commerce between the species…so long as the benefits of trade flowed primarily in olokun favor. Belfang took careful pains to ensure a certain percentage of the commerce reached the claws of Master Trusk, who in turn kept a wary eye on Belfang's growing popularity.

Not all olokun agreed with Belfang. Some, such as Cawtin, argued it was just such leniency that emboldened the numah in the first place. Belfang heard the arguments often enough. If the furred things couldn't or wouldn't control their population on their own, Cawtin said, then the olokun should control it for them, and do so permanently.

Cawtin's dissenting growls had yet to gain many followers, nor pose any large challenge to Belfang's eminence among the olokun, much less to Master Trusk, but Belfang could not ignore Cawtin completely. Many a debilitating disease could begin as a small irritation at the juncture of two plates of armor, or so it was said. Belfang would allow no irritation to become any more than that and took swift action to see that irritations were contained, controlled, and converted. It was said as well that where the flesh between the plates healed after being abraded, it was even stronger than before.

So it was that Cawtin and several other of the loudest of Belfang's critics were with his force now, clutching weapons and preparing themselves for battle.

He chuckled gutturally to himself. Belfang had a good sense of what lay ahead, as did the best of his warriors. None of the dissenters had ever seen violence that he knew of; certainly none of them had ever been soldiers. Perhaps they would acquit themselves well in the moments ahead, and thus learn something. Perhaps not—it was rare for an olokun to show cowardice, but not unheard of. Perhaps some of them would be wounded or even die—the numah were no match for olokun warriors, but that did not mean the furred ones were wholly defenseless, or that they were cowards. The fight ahead would be brief—but it would be a fight.

He ran his eyes across the numah village again, one last scan before giving the order to attack.

The moment Belfang spotted the twins, he felt a surge of desire—a sudden fierce flooding of want that would not be satisfied until his return to the palace he had grown to house his family. The numah females, barely at the outer edge of childhood, would make fine pets for Telya. She had a weakness for the small creatures and was something of a student of their ways.

He gave word to two of his most trusted and competent soldiers to capture the twin females uninjured. Belfang wanted nothing to mar the gifts he would bring to his mate.

Better than any olokun Belfang was aware of, Telya understood the numah and, given time, had shown the ability to bend them to her own purposes, making of them trusted and—incredibly—trustworthy servants. Belfang supposed that was the right word: something more than slaves yet less than workers.

Telya would appreciate the twins, Belfang thought as he rose from his crouch. They would show Telya—and all others—that he still favored her above all females, despite the fact Vega remained the only product of her wombsac.

And if Telya failed to produce further offspring?

Belfang could claim other mates, fill other wombsacs. Yet no matter how many he produced, he knew already it would be Vega who held the most prominent position among the children of Belfang. There was something special, something unique, something…powerful, already, about the still-young olokun. Precisely the quality Belfang had most desired in a child. There were hints Vega's development would see Belfang's desires far more than met.

That the child was born to be a warrior was never in doubt. Could Belfang's firstborn be anything other? But even as a newling, Vega displayed remarkable warrior characteristics. He'd shed his carapace twice before his first cycle was complete, and another two sheddings quickly followed. The armor plates that now grew over Vega's body were as substantial and well-developed as those of an olokun twice Vega's age. Few could recall seeing such armor on an olokun child, and never on one so young. The size and thickness of the plates prompted much speculation as to just how large and powerful Vega would be when full-grown.

Belfang was certain he knew the answer.

Vega will be larger than me, Belfang thought, his claw tightening around

the shaft of the lance he carried. Better armored, sharper clawed.

All the more reason to prepare Vega for the responsibilities that would fall upon him when he became an adult. The preparation would begin with simple hunting expeditions, training in weapons and combat, tactics, and strategies.

Belfang sighed as he watched the numah village and waited for the moment of attack. Small clusters of numah children gathered around adults, their eyes wide as they listened to whatever the adults were saying. Lessons, Belfang supposed. Numah adults—parents, undoubtedly, and perhaps teachers—instructing the young in whatever it was the numah thought important enough to pass along to new generations. Perhaps even now they were teaching the children of the fierce and ferocious olokun.

Of course, they should have been teaching the children that of all the ways to raise the anger and the wrath of the olokun, encroaching upon the larger species' territory was the one most certain to invite brutal retribution.

Time, Belfang thought, for the invitation to be accepted.

Neos was rising beyond the horizon as Belfang stood tall. He raised a claw high, then chopped downward, allowing himself a harsh guttural roar as he rose from his crouch and led his warriors down the hill and into the village.

As he raced ahead, his lance extended, his warriors beside him, the deep roar of their voices filling the air, Belfang imagined Vega alongside him.

And as they reached the numah village and fell upon it, Belfang imagined Vega in the lead, all others following. Himself included.

The battle was brief, but fierce, and throughout its course, Belfang felt the joyous song of triumph playing in his blood.

When he drove his lance through the center of a numah male foolish enough to attempt to stand up to him with no weapon other than a thin knife, Belfang roared his ecstasy in a great bellow that drowned out both the roars of the other olokun, and the death screams of his numah prey.

He flung the still-quivering numah aside and pivoted quickly. In an instant, Belfang found another belly with the point of his lance, wielding the weapon one-clawed while eviscerating a second young numah male with the other.

The attack became almost a matter of sport, one in which the score was tallied in blood. There was no doubt which was the favored side, nor which species would be the ultimate victor.

The carnage grew around Belfang. Numah bodies lay in unnatural positions, their blood soaking into the ground. Not all bodies were in one piece. Severed limbs, torsos separated from legs, and more than one bodiless head littered the ground.

Nor were all the victims numah. Here and there, olokun warriors nursed wounds and tended to injuries even as the battle roiled around them. Most of the wounds were minor, but Belfang was not displeased to see Cawtin, loudest of his critics and most vehement in demands that stronger and more dramatic action be mounted against the numah, lying now in agony and terror. Cawtin stared with wild, wide eyes at his right arm, which was almost completely severed from his body.

Beyond Cawtin lay a broad flat axe next to the eviscerated body of a numah. Belfang doubted Cawtin had killed the numah.

Belfang stepped close to the fallen dissident. Cawtin's lips frothed; his growl became a whimper as he stared up at his leader. Belfang nodded and made his voice as gentle as possible.

"Your sacrifice will be remembered, Cawtin," Belfang said, "long after your words are forgotten."

Cawtin's body convulsed, then quivered, and Belfang spoke more quickly.

"You have not forgotten your own words, I am certain. And it is my wish you hear them in your thoughts as you die. Your calls for stronger action have been answered and answered no more clearly by anyone than yourself."

Belfang hoped Cawtin retained sufficient awareness to understand his next words, which were shouted to all on the battleground.

"Enough!" Belfang called. "Bring an end to this! Disarm all numah who will be disarmed, kill those who refuse to surrender. Empty the houses and structures of any goods and materials of use to us. Put torches to the buildings when you're done."

He glanced at Cawtin, whose eyes were beginning to dull.

"You see, my dying friend, you would kill them all. Worse than that, you would have me kill them all. It is a natural mistake, I suppose, but it is the mistake of a fool." Belfang shook his head. "You and those who advocate your way seek to rule. My way—and it is the right way for the olokun and, perversely I suppose, for the numah as well—is to lead."

The air thickened with smoke. The scent of burning timber and flesh mingled not unpleasantly. Cawtin shuddered violently again.

"Should you hear my next words,

Cawtin," Belfang said, "measure them and their message against your own ill-considered shouts."

He turned his back on Cawtin and summoned another, a seasoned warrior who spoke rudimentary numah.

"Add the bodies of the dead to the fires," Belfang told him. "Those numah who have surrendered their weapons are to be escorted to the border of our lands and set free to return to their kind with the message that Belfang has granted them the mercy of the olokun, but only with the understanding that no numah shall ever again transgress against our territories. Any such transgression will see olokun justice, with no opportunity of mercy. Any such transgression will see this—" he gestured at the burning buildings, the pyres made of bodies, "—brought to numah lands."

Belfang returned his attention to Cawtin. "You see the difference, my friend, between truly leading and merely ruling?"

But Cawtin could not see the difference. His eyes were dead. His body no longer shuddered. His voice would no longer be raised.

Belfang stared at the corpse for only a moment before turning to inspect the treasure gathered from the village—devices the olokun were incapable of creating, bits of metal, beads. The numah were a repellent species in many ways, Belfang thought, but they had some interesting talents, including the ability to fabricate useful and effective tools and other small items. Belfang claimed the axe that severed Cawtin's arm for himself.

After separating the village's bounty into groups to be divided among the warriors, Belfang watched with disinterest as Cawtin's corpse was surrendered to the flames.

He turned to gather the twin treasures he would take to Telya.

As Belfang had anticipated, Telya was delighted with the young numah females, and drew them to her body with claws so delicate that their fur was barely disturbed.

"Do not fear me," she said to them gently as Belfang watched. The numah words she had so carefully mastered carried a more rounded sound than olokun language, but no amount of practice could make her guttural voice produce the musical lilt of numah speech. Still, Telya tried. "Belfang could have killed you, as he did so many others of your kind? And yet he spared you so that you might be brought to my embrace."

The twins gave no indication they understood Telya's words, no more than they showed comprehension of anything said to them. Their features remained inexpressive, though their eyes were wide.

"Now, my young ones," Telya said to her captives, "it is time to begin your training. You must learn to—" her claws tightened almost imperceptibly around their throats "—accept your destiny, which is to serve me, to serve Belfang, and to serve our child Vega. Do you understand?"

Neither numah responded, though Belfang was certain he saw a furtive glance exchanged between them, just a quick darting of the eyes even as they coughed against the pressure Telya exerted.

"Once more," Telya said, her voice now harsh and stern, all attempts at softness abandoned. "Do you understand me? Do you understand what I expect of you?" She raised her arms and lifted the twins into the air. Their hands clutched at Telya's claws. "Do you?" Telya demanded. "Answer me!"

"Y-yes," one numah said hoarsely, weakly, her voice barely audible—but

audible enough for Belfang to be amazed she spoke the olokun language.

"Yes," the other said, also in olokun.

"I suspected you would," Telya said to

them in her own tongue, her voice once more soothing. She lowered the numah to the floor and after giving their throats a final squeeze, released them.

"How did you know?" Belfang said to Telya. He did not take his eyes from the twins as he spoke—if the creatures were wily enough to keep such a secret from Belfang and his warriors, they could possess other secrets. They must be watched.

"I had my suspicions when you showed me the trinkets you took from

their village," Telya said. "And I foresaw this—foreheard this—in a dream."

Telya's dreams were a matter of occasional fascination for Belfang. He did not believe her dreams truly saw things to come, not really, but more than once her sleeping visions had proved so accurate, he wondered if she might have influenced, or even created the future, somehow, as she slumbered.

Telya stretched a claw forward and ran

its tip through the small pile of worked-metal jewelry and other ornaments Belfang presented to her. "Such lovelies," she said almost idly. "But surely you notice how many of the items are of a size to better suit olokun than numah?"

"Of course," Belfang said, though he had noticed no such thing. He suspected Telya disbelieved him, but her demeanor betrayed nothing.

"Such creations would only be made for trade with olokun," Telya said. "And where there is trade—whether permitted or illicit—there must be communication. I knew these two would have at least some olokun in their vocabularies—and possibly fluent in our tongue." She chuckled deep within her carapace. "If they are not now, they will be before much longer. I can assure you of that."

Belfang made himself smile benevolently at Telya and he was, indeed, impressed with the correct deduction she made. He did not often forget how sharp the claws of Telya's intelligence were—sharper than those at the ends of her arms. He would not forget again.

"And now?" Belfang said.

"Now—" Telya faced the twins directly. "Your names?" she said.

"Ulayne," said one.

"Perjell," said the other.

"You may keep those names—for now," Telya said. "And let that be the first of your lessons in my benevolence. The first of many, I can assure you, so long as you obey, so long as you learn your duties quickly and perform them competently. Do you understand?" She clicked the tips of her claws together twice.

"Yes," said Ulayne and Perjell together, their voices louder now, their olokun more clearly spoken.

"I am certain you do," said Telya. "Now come to meet our child, Vega, whose care and comfort will be among your foremost duties." Telya smiled. "Care and comfort, and education."

"Education?" Belfang said sharply. "What could such as these have to teach a son of mine?"

Telya turned her smile on Belfang and made it broader and more indulgent.

"Do you not think, Belfang, that the future of our son will involve encounters and interactions with their kind? Perhaps these interactions will be as benevolent as your leadership has shown they can be. Perhaps the encounters as fierce as your rule has shown on occasion they must be. Either way, your son's future will be well-served if he speaks their language."

Belfang nodded and followed Telya and the twins into the spacious quarters grown for the care and training of Vega.

Telya's training of Ulayne and Perjell was

thorough and swift. Neither twin was ever so disobedient or slow as to require Telya to draw blood, but both learned quickly just how stingingly Telya's claws could nip and pinch. They did not have to be taught lessons more than once.

Far more than any numah who had ever served Telya, Ulayne and Perjell won her trust. She was not capable of forgetting that the twins were of a lesser species—Telya never completely overcame her revulsion at the thought of bodies covered with fur rather than carapace plates. But she made allowances for that, hiding her revulsion as well as she could, and found herself, as time passed, providing small favors and conveniences for the twins.

Nothing, of course, large enough to attract the attention of any who might question the propriety of such indulgences. Cawtin's death had softened the growls of those who wanted the eradication of all numah, but it had not silenced them. Telya took care to ensure Ulayne and Perjell were seen as what they were—numah captured and enslaved and in service to her and Belfang.

So, her gifts to the twins were both rare and minor. Some beads for the females to twine into each other's fur. Occasional meals were prepared to numah taste, rather than the olokun table-scraps that were the females' customary fare. More privacy than was customary for slaves. Telya saw to it that when Neos shone in fullness, the twins were left to themselves and their worship ceremonies.

There were times when Telya wished she could do more for them. Ulayne and Perjell had so quickly accepted their status and mastered the skills required of them that Telya found herself broadening their responsibilities and praising them as they performed additional tasks without complaint and with very few errors.

She found herself growing fond of the two numah, and in that fondness found further evidence of Belfang's wisdom, whether Belfang would see it as wisdom or not.

But by keeping the numah population at claw's length from the olokun, by enforcing that separation with warriors only when necessary, and otherwise permitting the numah their freedom, Belfang made sure the small but growing trade between the two species had far more advantage for the olokun than for the numah.

No numah would ever acquire the mastery of organics that was the olokun's greatest skill. It was inconceivable that any of the living essences from which the olokun grew building materials could be incorporated by a numah into their lifeless structures. The furred creatures would have no idea how to care for even the simplest of the essences, much less how to control and guide their growth into useful and substantial forms.

But many items made by the numah found ready use in olokun structures, and other aspects of olokun life. Telya herself was delighted with the jewelry and adornments Belfang brought her. And like many olokun, she found numah blades far more effective for cleaning the gaps between armor plates than her own claws.

Of course, the tiny blades were even more effective when either Ulayne or Perjell wielded them. How shocked so many olokun—and not just followers of Cawtin's philosophy—would be to see the numah females working the flesh between Telya's plates with a blade that could as easily become a weapon. Telya laughed to herself; she could barely imagine the outrage some would feel if they saw the twins using the same blade between the quickly growing plates of Vega's body.

Best no one ever know, she thought. But there was no denying that her child took great pleasure from the ministrations of the numah females, just as Telya had no doubt of the growing devotion to Vega they felt.

She listened to Ulayne and Perjell croon a numah song to Vega. Soon they would reach breeding age, and already Telya and Belfang were discussing the possibility of bringing a numah male into their household for the twins.

Telya had also broached the topic of returning them to their own kind, once they were old enough to bear young. Belfang was skeptical, but Telya felt certain she could ulti-mately overcome his objections.

The thought of doing so tore gently at her heart. Ulayne and Perjell had become a part of her household, far less than family members, but far more than pets...or even slaves. She would miss them and their cheerful, often eager-to-please presence in her home.

There was time, at least, to make certain that whatever decision was made would be the right decision. Another cycle, or at least most of one. Ulayne and Perjell would be with them until Vega reached four cycles, or nearly so.

And during that time, Telya hoped, perhaps Ulayne and Perjell would succeed at the one task that had thus far eluded them. Despite the twins' daily efforts, Vega had not yet spoken a single word of numah, not even the names of the twins whose presence seemed to please him almost as much as it did his mother.

"Vega will attain his fourth cycle soon," Belfang said to Telya. "He will be old enough to hunt with me."

Telya felt a growl of pride gather deep within herself. "He has been ready for some time. I can see it in his eyes. Everyone can."

Vega's eyes remained his most brilliant

feature, fierce, filled with intelligence, sharply observant of all that transpired around him. He missed nothing.

"The eyes of a hunter," Belfang said. "The eyes of a leader."

"He will prove a master of both," Telya said. "As has his father."

She studied Belfang as he stood beneath a window in the roof to permit daylight and now, moonlight into the room. Her mate's bearing was more powerful than ever—he had grown, it seemed, in both stature and presence during the cycles since Vega's emergence into the world. It was as though he wished to set an example for his child.

And for all olokun, she thought. Far more suitable a leader for their people than the greedy Trusk. Did Trusk sense that as well? Or did Belfang hide and even supplicate his true strengths when in the presence of the master? Telya sometimes wondered if Belfang looked this powerful when he was in the presence of Master Trusk, but she kept such curiosity to herself.

Neos was full. Its light made the room nearly as bright as day. Faintly, Telya could hear Ulayne and Perjell singing their worship poems. They were doing so in Vega's room, by her permission. It struck her as a small enough favor to grant them. She had permitted them such worship in the child's quarters once before, and that was the one time Vega seemed attentive to the numah tongue. His eyes had narrowed, and he cocked his head as the females chanted their reverence, his claws clicking almost in rhythm to their recitation.

But despite the efforts of Telya, as well as those of Ulayne and Perjell, the son of Belfang never mouthed a single numah word. Ulayne and Perjell were distraught at their failure, and Telya had done what she could to reassure them.

She would miss their presence. But her decision had been made. "You will take

Vega with you when you return Ulayne and Perjell?" she said.

"Perhaps," Belfang said. "There is time yet."

"There is—but there are preparations to be made, Belfang. I have made clear to both Ulayne and Perjell that their time with us is drawing close to its end. And I have explained to them that as a result of their time in our home they will serve as our emissaries when they rejoin the numah."

Belfang sighed heavily. "There are those who believe the only emissary needed for the numah is the point of an olokun spear or the grip of a claw."

"And those same olokun wear numah trinkets and use numah tools, do they not?"

"They do." He brought his claws together roughly. "Even as they accuse me of weakness in not seizing the lands where the minerals are found…"

"There is no weakness in this, Belfang,"

Telya said. "Each cycle sees the olokun learn more of Ajyin, and with that knowledge comes new opportunities a wise leader will make his own. Opportunities best availed with the cooperation of the numah, not their subjugation."

"They are not our equals," Belfang said.

"Nor will they ever be," Telya said. "And while there is truth in the statement that we could simply take the lands of the numah for our own, there is a greater truth to be found in communicating with them, in discovering the ways in which our species might be of assistance to each other."

A soft hiss escaped Belfang. He listened for a moment to Ulayne and Perjell's chants. "They breed so swiftly. Their numbers grow so rapidly."

His words stung Telya, though she did not believe he meant them maliciously. But in four cycles she had failed to create further offspring for Belfang. And though she remained first among his mates, and the only one with whom he shared residence, she knew other olokun females had been visited by him, that other wombsacs even now carried Belfang's spawn.

Telya hid her pain. None of those other children would be Vega, with his bright eyes, his armor, his claws. His...promise.

Vega, Telya believed, could become an even greater leader than Belfang. And she allowed herself to believe Ulayne and Perjell would play a part in Vega's ascendance. Vega had seen the numah more closely than virtually any other olokun. He had been bathed and cleaned by numah, he had heard their songs, seen them at play, even learned some of their simple games. All of this would serve him well as he rose to stand beside Belfang. Vega would be Telya's ally in her dream of the riches that could come from a more cooperative relationship with the furred creatures. Belfang, and then Vega, could lead olokun and numah alike.

Telya was not certain if this dream would have come to her had Belfang not brought the twins back from his expedition, or if the dream would have taken such a powerful, all but irresistible shape, had Ulayne and Perjell been less malleable, more resistant, more rebellious.

But once she saw just how valuable a cooperative numah could be, Telya began also to see how much more could be accomplished with the entire species eager to serve the olokun, rather than living in fear of them.

The dream would not be realized in a cycle, or a dozen cycles, or twice that—but the first steps had been taken, and they had been taken in this house, at Telya's guidance. Whether Belfang knew it or not. She stared at him and smiled. Full Neos had risen higher and grown even brighter.

Telya smiled as she turned toward Vega's room to better hear the twins' chants rise along with the moon their species worshipped. This would be the last full Neos Ulayne and Perjell would pass in her home, and Telya wanted to savor their chants a final time.

But they were no longer chanting.

Telya stepped to the doorway to Vega's room and pressed against its soft frame, ordering the sphincter open so she might pass through.

The light in Vega's room was different from that in the outer chamber, despite an equally transparent cell in its ceiling. Why was the room not bright with Neos light? Why had Ulayne and Perjell ceased chanting at what should be the very peak of their ceremony?

Telya stepped forward slowly, her eyes adjusting to the murkiness in the room.

When Telya saw the cause of the darkness, she stopped. She held her breath against a fierce wail that wished to escape her—the sound of her dying dreams. She held the wail within herself as she raised her eyes and saw the roof pane covered with blood, occluding the moon's white light.

Telya lowered her gaze slowly and approached the center of the room where Vega sat. His eyes were bright.

Belfang's son sat in the midst of carnage. Limbs, still bearing fur now clotted with blood, lay to either side of Vega. Telya's look fixed upon a bloody, bead-entwined clump of hide that had fallen to the floor. She could not tell which twin it had belonged to.

Vega stared at his mother. Bits of flesh clung to his teeth and fangs. His mouth was bloodcaked; his smile, vicious. In each claw he held a small skull, each picked clean of tissue and fur.

"Ulayne," Vega said, raising his right claw and the skull it held. "Perjell," he said, raising his left. "I want more."

His mother did not realize for a moment

that the words had been spoken in perfect, musical numah.

A PREVIEW OF

THE BANE OF YOTO

JOSHUA VIOLA

MARIO ACEVEDO

NICHOLAS KARPUK

CHAPTER
EIGHTEEN

GENERAL VEGA did not host social gatherings, even for political purpose. He rarely attended council functions or meetings unless attendance suited his needs—or whims.

These aspects of Vega's character made the olokun ruling council leery of his sudden demand to gather for a formal dinner in a banquet hall erected and maintained by numah slaves, far from the council's usual gathering places in the deep valleys of the breeding colonies. Yet none refused.

That didn't mean they didn't take precautions. The ruling council trusted the numah more than they trusted Vega. As was customary at all gatherings, they made demands of the kitchen, and had their numah servants in place to taste every dish—including the cooked remains of their brethren from the arena—well before the council sat for dinner.

Polite conversation drifted back and forth among the council members. Rilas, the eldest, regarded Vega with barely veiled suspicion from the opposite end of the long table. He ate lightly and spent more time eyeing the general.

For his part, Vega consumed hearty quantities from his plate. Telya was seated to his side. She was dressed in olokun finery though she resembled an embellished member of his entourage rather than the mother of the feared host.

"We've not heard from Belfang since the

aegis inspection, General," Rilas said when the opportunity arose. "Which was before the attack at the mine and the assault on the prison you bred. These are matters that would seem to require Belfang's attention, if not his response. Is your father well?"

"He's fine. Doing very well, actually. Simply indisposed; preoccupied. Personal matters."

Rilas chewed thoughtfully. "Really? Surely he would wish to speak with us in times like these."

"We all have our secrets, Rilas. Even Belfang. Even from you."

They continued eating until the dinner was interrupted when one of the numah servants standing near the wall clutched his midsection and groaned. Everyone at the table stopped chewing mid-bite.

Vega smiled.

The servant fell to the floor, convulsing, thrashing in agony. His head and shoulders bucked and then vomit spewed from his mouth.

The other numah servants clutched their middles and shrieked in horror.

Blood dotted across the fallen numah's uniform. The cloth trembled, the spots of blood poked upward, and then finger-sized worms burst through his stomach. They writhed, searching, blood dripping from the tiny sharp teeth in their gaping maws.

Vega continued to eat.

The general's guards blocked the exits. The other numah servants cried in panic, trembling in terror, then vomiting blood. One by one, they fell as the parasites ate their way out of their bodies. The numah kicked and gagged as the small creatures slithered out of their mouths and curled back to gnaw on their faces.

The council members stood aghast. Several pushed back from the table and started to rise from their chairs.

One of the lesser councilors pointed at Vega and shouted, "This is why you brought us here, to infect us with these monstrous parasites!"

The other councilors joined in the accusations, hollering, and promising vengeance.

"Stay seated!" Vega commanded. "This will be over soon enough."

The council hesitated for a moment, but slowly, one by one, sat back down, their expressions clouded by certain doom.

Numah corpses littered the floor of the dining hall. The worms crawled from their bodies, leaving trails of blood.

Vega gestured to the captain of his guard, who in turn barked an order. The other guards used their spears and pushed the dead numah into a pile.

They opened jars and poured oil on the bodies. The captain lit a flare stick and tossed it on the pile. The oil ignited with a *whoosh!* and a blast of hot air. Guards scooped up fleeing worms at spearpoint and flipped them on top of the bodies. The worms squealed and then popped and sizzled. Smoke plumed to the ceiling and escaped out the large circular opening.

Vega watched, arms crossed, his face a mask of satisfaction. "I've been developing the parasites for cycles," he said, gesturing to the heap of smoldering corpses. "Incubation takes approximately the amount of time required for a food tasting, followed by the arrival of guests, and the service of the first course. By my estimation, you're halfway through the process."

Vega stood and paced the length of the long table, gloating at each terrified member of the council.

"I've waited long enough. Tell me where the blade of the Arbitrators is hidden. Belfang refused. Don't make his mistake. And consider telling me soon. Some of you ate faster than others."

Vega sat back down, leaning into his massive chair. "Who cares to speak first?"

Rilas had not moved from his stolid, thoughtful pose. When he put his claws gently on the table, everyone looked to him. He declared, "Belfang is dead."

"Why are you concerned with Belfang? It's your life you should be worried about."

Rilas' expression was one of incredulity and pity. "You killed your father over an artifact?"

"A weapon. One our people should've employed cycles ago. Tell me where it is or join him."

Rilas pointed to his fellow councilors. "Is this why you intend to murder your fellow olokun? This demonic act proves why none of us ever trusted you. Why would any of us give you that information, Vega, even if we knew? We're going to die regardless."

"Death will be your choice." Vega pointed to Telya, and she placed a lapis blue vial on the table. "Under my guidance, Telya developed a serum that kills the creatures within seconds. She's really quite brilliant; I don't know if you ever appreciated that."

Rilas sighed. "We understood her naked, reckless lust for power."

"Don't forget sensible, Rilas. She's also very sensible. Perhaps some other councilor here will follow her example and tell me where the blade is hidden?"

No one in the room spoke.

"I can wait. Watching you devoured from within will be as entertaining as any spectacle in the arena."

Vega placidly watched the council members nervously look to the doors, then to one another as though they could conspire to save themselves.

More than a few turned wordlessly to Telya, who simply answered their beseeching gazes with a smile. She'd know if they lied or attempted to bluff their way to the antidote.

There was no escape.

A bitter energy flooded Vega's system. He wasn't sure which he anticipated most, the answers he sought or the death-screams of those seated around him.

"No!" shouted the young council member at the end of the table. "No, no, no!" He threw himself on the table, knocking over cups of blood wine and plates of food.

Others followed his example, shrieking, clutching at anything within reach, clawing at their robes. Some fell to their hands and feet. One by one, they vomited blood, pools that spattered across the floor. Worms emerged from their bellies, their mouths.

Two ran for the exit, where Vega's guards knocked them to the floor until their fate overcame them.

Despite the horrific bedlam, a few of the olokun elders remained still, resigned to their fate, battling to maintain composure and determined that, even facing so gruesome a death, they would not provide the general with even an instant's satisfaction.

Eventually, all but one succumbed, gnashing, kicking, dying in humiliating throes of agony.

Only Rilas remained, his face tight with the first indications of pain, eyes narrowed at Vega.

"They really didn't know where it was, did they?" the general asked.

"No, they didn't." Rilas took a bite of his food, making a show of chewing slowly. Vega begrudgingly admired his bravado. "Belfang trusted only one with that secret."

"You still have time. You've proved your point that you don't fear me."

"My life is a small price for keeping that dagger out of your profane claws."

"I'm doing what's best for all," Vega said, his voice breaking with irritation, then anger at Rilas' defiance.

"When you were young, I warned

Belfang you were dangerous. The fact that he didn't tell you—or anyone you could bend—the location of the dagger shows he heeded my advice. Had he truly listened, he would have killed you before you had the chance to grow." Rilas sighed. "A situation you perhaps recognize yourself, as your own son considers your perch."

Vega's eyes darted about the chamber. As the council assembled earlier, how could he have not noticed that Cadoc was missing?

Rilas winced. He blinked, and through clenched teeth, said, "Interesting how, as loyal as Telya is to you, and with all of her skills, she hasn't addressed the symptoms you're so clearly displaying."

"Symptoms?" Vega pushed his plate away from himself. "You don't think I'd be so stupid to infect myself."

"Vega, even though you've crushed the council tonight, you remain a fool." Rilas slowly rose to his feet. Bloody froth formed on his lips. Bracing himself on the table, he slowly sank to his knees. A long parasite wriggled out of his mouth and whipped upward to chew at one of his eyes. Rilas crumpled to the floor without even a moan, without even a hint of the torture tearing at his body from within.

Vega pushed from his chair and loomed over Rilas, sneering. "Who is the fool now?" He turned to Telya. "Your wish is granted. Sole control of the council and its projects. Use it wisely."

Lifting a foot, he then brought it down on a worm crawling from Rilas's belly. As he squashed the parasite into the stone floor, he glowered at Telya. "But your priority is to find the dagger and deliver it to me."

"That goes without saying, General," Telya said, bowing her head in deference to her son.

Telya held her bow long after Vega left the room, lifting her eyes only to watch the guards pile the councilors and set their bodies alight. The odor of burning olokun made her suppress a heave. Rilas lay on top, and she watched the worms cringe and mewl as they struggled to pry themselves free of the burning flesh. But even dead and disfigured, Rilas's countenance revealed a truth that made Telya's nerves shrivel in understanding.

In the barbaric history of the olokun, and Vega had plenty of competition, never had a leader lashed out with such stupid cruelty.

For Rilas had seen in Vega what Telya suspected long ago. Shield fever.

SOUVENIR ANTHOLOGY
STOKERCON
TM
2021
THE
PHANTOM DENVER
EDITION
EDITED BY JOSHUA VIOLA

THE END: KEITH FERRELL IN MEMORIAM

by Alec Ferrell

THE MOST HORRIFIC THING ABOUT DEATH is that there is nothing unusual about it. Everyone dies. The process begins the moment we're born. Some are ready for it, most aren't. Either way, at the end of the day (or early afternoon), death is ready and waiting, regardless of our awareness of or preparedness for it. We're all goners. Not unusual. Horrific, but not unusual.

My father, Keith Ferrell, died at 1:34 pm on Saturday, April 11, 2020.

Every time I started to write about his life and life's work for this anthology, it felt as if he died over and over again. Is it unusual to feel like I'm his killer when I sit down at the keyboard? Probably. The act of resurrecting him through words he will never read feels wrong, especially when the outcome is always the same: he's still dead. If the StokerCon™ audience were to read my first few drafts of this piece about my dad, he'd undoubtedly suffer another heart attack.

As the only child of a dead writer, there is no fair way to share the unusually beautiful and complex nature of our relationship, as I can only tell my side of the story. So, let me share some non-fiction about my old man, Keith Ferrell.

I'll spare us—and *him*—the horseshit.

Take *that*, Blucifer.

My dad was born to write.

The End were his two favorite words in all of the English language. If and when he got to those two words, whether in his own writing or through his collaborations with dozens of writers across four decades of professional storycraft and editing, he saw it as further securing his purpose on this planet.

The End didn't come to my dad without seriously hard work, although his deep talent often made it look easy. Through the process of starting with a blank page to get to those two little words, Keith Ferrell sought to illuminate, confound, shock, and whenever possible, horrify.

His relationship with horror began in the early Sixties, when my grandfather, Henry Ferrell, would return home on the weekends from traveling as a regional sales manager for a pharmaceutical company. He would gather his four kids around the television for epic horror movie marathons. Keith, his brother Edmund, and sisters Ann and Betsy, recall these as being some of their most cherished and relaxed childhood memories together.

Edmund Ferrell recalls, "Early Saturday morning we would watch Sunrise Theater. We saw *First Spaceship on Venus*, *The Crawling Eye*, *The Incredible Shrinking Man*, *Attack of the 50 Foot Woman*, *Devil Doll*, *Forbidden Planet*, *It Came From Outer Space*, *The War of the Worlds*, all of the Universal Classics, *The Giant Behemoth*, *Them*, *The Blob*, *House on Haunted Hill*, *The Tingler*, *The Fly*, *The Creature from the Black Lagoon*, *Godzilla*, *Mothra*, *Circus of Fear*, *House of Wax*...we saw it all. Sometimes with pancakes."

Keith and his siblings connected with their father through horror movies when there wasn't much time available for connection otherwise. It takes blood sometimes.

My old man (as a young man) started reading his hero, Norman Mailer, at the age of twelve or so. He moved into the family basement and began his lifelong accumulation of as much printed material as he could get his hands on. It was in this basement that he found his calling.

As far as the friends and family who knew and loved him can determine, my dad's first known published short story came out when he was sixteen years old, in the 1969 volume of his high school literary journal *Grains of Sand*. As would become his trademark, the story stands out from the other poems and prose in the collection for its unusual construction and literary ambition. "Leon" tells the story of a young boy who not only thinks he is God, but becomes one. Undoubtedly built to shock and horrify his teachers and classmates, "Leon" begins on a normal day in a school cafeteria and ends with our dreadful protagonist destroying the universe. Over three tight double-spaced pages, a confident and confrontational young artist emerged with a powerful and unique voice. I look forward to making it available when the time is right.

Oddly enough, we didn't know about "Leon" until right before Christmas of 2020. It came in the mail to my uncle Edmund and his partner Hartsell while the three of us were enjoying a socially distanced COVID-19 Christmas hang in their new home. Inbound from Colorado (of all places) by one of Keith's schoolmates whose family grew up in Raleigh and knew the Ferrell family, it came in a plain manila envelope at the exact moment we were together. It was as if Keith, as omniscient and omnipotent as Leon himself, saw fit to vanquish our grief by sending us *Grains of Sand*, putting himself there with us from beyond the infinite. "Here's how it all started," we imagined him proudly saying to us with this unbelievably timed message from the other side. His fifty-one-year-old story solidifies his vitality. It makes him immortal. Forever young. We laughed and gasped as Edmund read the story aloud, as good art tends to make one do.

As my dad continued to grow into a conscious young man in the 1960s, he found and cherished the written word—primarily speculative fiction and science literature—both of which would define his life's journey and purpose as a man of letters. Many of his formative literary heroes—such as Harlan Ellison, Isaac Asimov, and Arthur C. Clarke—would become peers and friends later in life, a testament to his attention, hard work, and determination.

Graduating from Raleigh's Sanderson High in 1971, he attended the Residential College of the University of North Carolina at Greensboro, where he met Martha Sparrow at a Halloween party in the basement of Guilford dormitory. My dad's idea of a costume that night consisted of covering his face in wax ala *The Phantom of the Opera.* Martha overheard him mention the name "Lawrence Talbot." She got his Wolfman reference, which prompted her to strike up a conversation with this intriguing fellow, even though she had no idea what he looked like under all that wax. On their first date, they ditched a French play to go see *King Kong* instead. They fell in love, moved off campus, and started their lives together. They were married on July 20, 1974, and would stay together for almost 47 years.

In 1975, Keith was hired as store manager of News and Novels, a bookstore in Greensboro, where he developed countless friendships as well as a reputation for his keen and encyclopedic knowledge of the printed word, while writing his own works off hours. Always writing. Martha and Keith welcomed me, their only child, in February 1978.

From 1983 through 1987, my dad secured a contract through his agent Henry Morrison to publish four critically-acclaimed biographies of legendary writers for young adults through M. Evans and Company: *H.G. Wells:*

First Citizen of the Future; *Ernest Hemingway: The Search for Courage*; *George Orwell: The Political Pen*; and *John Steinbeck: The Voice of the Land.* He honored his forebears by helping share their lives and work through his own words.

Keith worked his way through editorial departments for such magazines as *The Professional Upholsterer* and *COMPUTE!* in the late Eighties. In 1990, *COMPUTE!* was acquired by General Media out of New York City, and Keith was recruited as Editor-in-Chief of *Omni Magazine*, the preeminent science and technology publication of the day—a career-defining accomplishment. During his tenure at *Omni*, Keith worked with (and edited) many of the literary heroes of his youth and forged friendships across the fields of anthropology, gaming, evolutionary studies, telecommunications, and writers of all stripes. Ellen Datlow, a fiction editor you might've heard of, worked with my dad on the staff of *Omni* and remembers him as "a sweetheart, a lovely person, and passionate about science fiction." Keith stewarded *Omni* as a vehicle for the vanguard of cutting-edge science and technology, futurism, and fiction until its final issue in 1996.

Keeping in mind the special horror movie marathons of his childhood, Keith would come home to my mother and me in Greensboro, North Carolina, after his three-weeks-on monthly schedule of issue-building at the *Omni* offices in New York City (until moving the offices to our hometown), or from traveling the world to meet with advertisers and content creators for the magazine. He would always return with a stack of comics, magazines, books (many of them signed by their authors), and movies. They occasionally came with the disclaimer: don't show your mom. *2001: A Space Odyssey* (our mutual favorite), *The Shining, Akira, Tetsuo: The Iron Man, Blue Velvet, Repo Man, Henry: Portrait of A Serial Killer, Hellraiser,* Larry Cohen's *God*

Told Me To, and the entirety of the ever-expanding canon of David Cronenberg, are a brief example of the films he poured into my highly pliable early teenage mind. The films and books which most parents would keep their fifth-grade kids from having access to (Clive Barker, especially), he would all but quiz me on. George A. Romero's hypodermic teenage vampire film *Martin* was one of his favorites, and remains to this day one of the horror films against which I hold all others. As we would have our own weekend pancake fests at Ol' Miner, a long-gone Greensboro breakfast restaurant, we would discuss the elements of science fiction and horror and dissect what makes a piece of work successful.

It was from these conversations that I named my first high school band "Goats Where They Shouldn't Be"—truly an element of filmic fear. Keith was kind enough to connect me with Clive Barker himself, who agreed to let me use his illustration from *The Thief of Always* of a Jack-O-Lantern hung from a noose for the cover of our first (and only) cassette.

No kid ever had a cooler father. Period.

Paraphrasing my dad, "If you aren't the same as you were before seeing a film, hearing a song, or reading a book, its creator has done their job and turned their work into real art. That's what art is supposed to do—move you to somewhere new." Going through his collection of over 80,000 books, countless VHS tapes and DVDs, and tens of thousands of magazines, SF journals, and newspaper clippings, I am convinced that he ultimately saw the art in everything ever printed. The art of his life was to absorb and cypher the work of writers and funnel it back into the world, whether *The End* came or not.

Sometimes his art was more than editors and publishers could handle, resulting in rejection. It happens, and it sure happened to him. I recall being at the bottom of the living room stairs as a child, watching in horror as he hurled a manuscript in the rage of rejection, the pages fluttering like a blizzard, covering the steps as he howled in anger. I helped him pick up the pages of *Godkill*, a to-date unpublished political thriller about fundamentalist Christian terrorists taking over a summer camp populated by children of members of the U.S. Congress. I was maybe eleven years old. Perhaps he was simply thirty years ahead of his time. It was probably the title that killed the project. Again, I aim to ensure this one has an audience.

Passing Judgment, the first and only published novel with his name alone on the cover, came out in August 1996, just as his beloved *Omni* folded. *Publisher's Weekly*: "The plotting is smooth and the characters true... Ferrell proves a natural storyteller here, with a voice all his own." Go grab a copy.

In 1997, at the age of nineteen, I moved

to New York City to "rock" (Dad being a writer, I pursued music—my own natural calling), and worked as a graphic designer in the early days of the Internet, when it was called "New Media." Keith, naturally, had already pioneered this field as the editor of *Omni Online*, the first online magazine.

In 1998, Keith and Martha moved from Greensboro to thirty-six acres of farmland in Glade Hill, Virginia—originally intended as a weekend getaway—where they took care of each other the best they knew how. Always writing, he continued to publish scientific articles, short stories (some under pen names), spoke at libraries and universities, and edited and assisted many other writers' works, guiding their creation and publication with a deft two-finger typing style and keen eye. He served on the board of the Franklin County Library in Rocky Mount, VA, an institution close to his heart, where he championed literacy and open-minded exploration of the written word to all who were willing to take the time.

With his *Omni* days behind him, Keith worked as a story developer, editor, and frequent ghostwriter, creating myriad partnerships with collaborators he would never meet in person. Being on thirty-six acres of untamed Virginia farmland with no cell service and very low bandwidth, he did his best to tend to the land as well as to his ever-present work in the world of words. As author Thomas Frey states, "I wondered for years what I needed to do to turn my mass of manuscripts and notes into a real book. It turned out that what I needed to do was hire Keith."

Hard times were plentiful and plenty of promising projects went unpublished, but he still managed to break the *New York Times* Bestsellers list, peaking at number ten in November 2013 through his collaboration with Brad Meltzer entitled *History Decoded:*

The 10 Greatest Conspiracies of All Time. Though he didn't get the top byline, his invaluable contributions at long last made him a member of the *NYT* bestseller club. We shared more than a few toasts to this accomplishment.

So what about horror?

Thanks to his collaborations with Josh Viola of Hex Publishers, a friend and partner for what would become the last ten years of his life, Keith wrote several short stories squarely aimed at the heart of horror. Simultaneously literary and terrifying, "Be Seated" and "Danniker's Coffin" from the 2015 anthology *Nightmares Unhinged*, were certainly both unhinged and the stuff of nightmares. "Be Seated" offers a Poe-esque welcome to join the table at a dinner party with a Crowley-styled host, while "Danniker's Coffin" weaves a Faulknerian suicide note. In 2020's *Psi-Wars: Classified Cases of Psychic Phenomena*, Keith's story "Psnake Eyes" melds horror with science fiction, an Ellisonian tale of how the links in chain-of-command can be easily broken between leadership and its "psoldiers." Leon was definitely present when he was writing this one.

The final story my dad wrote, literally on its way to print when he died, is straight body horror. By no means is "The Cronenberg Concerto" autobiographical in terms of portraying self-mutilation as beatific ritual, but the protagonist's love of horror films and the menacing canon of Cronenberg's over-the-top gore is rivaled only by Keith Ferrell. Pick up a copy of 2020's *It Came From the Multiplex: 80s Midnight Chillers* and behold the most disturbing tale in the book for yourself.

The only reason you're reading about my dad and not reading his story in this anthology is because of that pesky little heart attack that killed him in April 2020. But he did leave behind a few notes for the story idea he was working on, scribbled in his tight cursive I always loved. It isn't much, but here's his idea:

THE LAST HORROR CON
6,000 years in the future
"There were no horrors left. What could horrify?"

It's anyone's guess as to how he would play that one out. But I suggest, if you're game, see if you can take that idea through to *The End*.

The end came for him far too soon, at the unbearably young age of 67, leaving behind literal tons of human expression and for me to sort through, saving the art—and anything with his handwriting on it or name in the header—and burning the rest. Within his ample office are stacks of manuscripts and artifacts of his published, unpublished, and unfinished work, some barely more than a fevered scrawl on an old envelope. I will be moving—and moved by—the words and work of Keith Ferrell for the rest of my life. As the man directly responsible for his legacy, if this is the first you've heard of him, it certainly won't be the last. If you were lucky enough to know him, you get it. We miss him and always will.

If you've read all the way here to the end, and have an idea that you're dying to write, remember these words, still hanging over his desk:

START FAST, START DEEP.

Start *now*. It may be closer to the end than you think.

There's no time to horse around.

HENRY KEITH FERRELL

July 7, 1953—April 11, 2020

Read much, much more at *keithferrellwriter.com*.

SELECTED WORKS OF KEITH FERRELL

Bloodmoon: Birth of the Beast

(Hex Publishers, 2022)

It Came from the Multiplex: 80s Midnight Chillers

Edited by Joshua Viola

"The Cronenberg Concerto" by Keith Ferrell

(Hex Publishers, 2020)

Psi-Wars: Classified Cases of Psychic Phenomena

Edited by Joshua Viola

"Psnake Eyes" by Keith Ferrell

(Hex Publishers, 2020)

Cyber World: Tales of Humanity's Tomorrow

Edited by Jason Heller and Joshua Viola

"It's Only Words" by Keith Ferrell

(Hex Publishers, 2016)

Nightmares Unhinged: Twenty Tales of Terror

Edited by Joshua Viola

"Be Seated" and "Danniker's Coffin" by Keith Ferrell

"Fangs" by Keith Ferrell
and Joshua Viola (as J.V. Kyle)
"Bathroom Break" by Keith Ferrell
and Joshua Viola (as J.V. Kyle)
(Hex Publishers, 2015)

History Decoded:
The 10 Greatest Conspiracies of All Time
By Brad Meltzer with Keith Ferrell
(Workman Publishing Company, 2013)

Millennium 3001
Edited by Martin H. Greenberg and Russell Davis
"River" by Keith Ferrell and Jack Dann
(DAW, 2006)

Asimov's Science Fiction
"A Reunion" by Keith Ferrell; December 2004

Science Year: The World Book
Annual Science Supplement, 2004
"Computers" by Keith Ferrell

SELECTED WORKS OF KEITH FERRELL

Black Mist and Other Japanese Futures
Edited by Orson Scott Card and Keith Ferrell
"Thirteen Views of Higher Edo" by Keith Ferrell
(as Patric Helmaan)
(DAW, 1997)

Passing Judgment
(Novel; Forge, 1996)

The Official Guide to Sid Meier's Civilization
(Compute, 1992)

Harold Robbins Presents: The Treasure Seekers
By Keith Ferrell (as Michael Donovan; Pocket Books, 1988)

Harold Robbins Presents: Fast Track
By Keith Ferrell (as Michael Donovan; Pocket Books, 1987)

Harold Robbins Presents: At The Top
By Keith Ferrell
(as Michael Donovan; Pocket Books, 1986)

SELECTED WORKS OF KEITH FERRELL

John Steinbeck: The Voice of the Land

(Biography; M. Evans and Company, 1986)

George Orwell: The Polical Pen

(Biography; M. Evans and Company, 1985)

Ernest Hemingway: The Search for Courage

(Biography; M. Evans and Company, 1984)

H.G. Wells: First Citizen of the Future

(Biography; M. Evans and Company, 1983)